Crabby Swims Free

HAPPY READING!
This book is especially for:

Lillian

Suzanne Tate,
Author—
brings fun and
facts to us in her
Nature Series.

James Melvin,
Illustrator—
brings joyous life
to Suzanne Tate's
characters.

Suzanne and James in costume

Crabby Swims Free
A Tale of a Close Call
Suzanne Tate
Illustrated by James Melvin

Nags Head Art

To Everett
(1924-2008)
whose loving support
will always be with me

National Award Winner
in the National Federation of Press Women's
2009 Communications Contest

Library of Congress Control Number 2008909244
ISBN 978-1-878405-55-5
ISBN 1-878405-55-1
Published by
Nags Head Art, Inc., P.O. Box 2149, Manteo, NC 27954
Copyright© 2008 by Nags Head Art, Inc.

Crabby and Nabby were two lively crabs.
Their shells were bright and colorful.
HUMANS called them "beautiful swimmers."

Crabby's claws were big and strong.
He could catch and eat lots
of little fish.

The fishy food made Crabby grow fast.
One day he became too big for his shell.

Crabby was about to pop open!
"Will you help me find a place to hide?"
he asked his friend, Nabby.

"We'd better find one before you 'bust'
and become a soft crab," replied Nabby.

Now Nabby was a she-crab or "sook."
She had shed her shell many times as she grew.

Nabby knew the danger in being a soft crab.
"Everything likes to eat a crab
when it is soft," she said.

Crabby and Nabby looked for a place
for him to hide.
"Oh, here's a nice dark hole," Crabby said,
and he crawled right in!

"I'll come with you," said Nabby.
And she crawled in too.

But that dark hole was a crab pot!
A crabber had placed it in the water
to catch crabs that would soon shed.

It was quiet and peaceful in the pot.
Crabby and Nabby thought that
they were safe.

Suddenly, a crabber came along
in his big boat!
"I wonder how many 'crawl-ins' are
in this pot today," he thought.

He pulled in the pot with his strong arms.
"Only two crabs," he sighed when
he saw Crabby and Nabby.

The crabber dumped the crabs
into a basket in his boat.

Other crabby crabs were there too.
"Oh, I don't like this at all," cried Crabby.
"I'm scared too," said Nabby.

The crabber ran his boat fast until he came to a dock.
Then he carried the basket of crabs
to a crab tank.

The crabber lifted up each crab and looked
at it carefully. He frowned when he saw Nabby.

"This one is an old 'sook' crab," the crabber said.
"She won't shed her shell again."
And he tossed her back into the water.

"But here's a nice 'buster.' It will soon shed its shell," the crabber said as he picked up Crabby. "Into the tank you go!"

At first, Crabby felt good in the tank.
He was happy to be covered with water
and glad that Nabby was free.

That night, Crabby's shell opened wider and wider.
He pulled out of his shell — backwards!

Crabby felt weak and flimsy.
It was a lot of work to shed his shell.
He felt so tired.

But soon his soft shell began
to fill out and become firm.

Early in the morning, Miss Dottie Crabsitter
came to the tank to check the crabs.
"This crab is a papershell — its shell is getting hard,"
she said when she picked up Crabby.

Carefully, Miss Dottie placed Crabby
in a box with other soft crabs.
Then she put the box in a cold room
called a cooler.

Crabby soon became cold too — he could hardly
move his claws and legs.

A little later, Miss Dottie walked into the cooler
and picked up the box with Crabby.
"Time to go to Capt. Mickey's," she said.

She carried Crabby's box and several others
and put them in an old blue truck.

The truck bounced on the winding road.
Miss Dottie soon came to Capt. Mickey's Crabhouse.
It was a busy place!

A woman took Miss Dottie's box out of the truck.
"This one is a papershell," she said
when she picked up Crabby.

NYC

"But a crab with a firm shell will get to New York City better than if he is too soft."
"New York City!" thought Crabby.
"Will I ever see Nabby again?"

Slowly, Crabby began to warm up in the box.
He could move his claws
and legs again.

A little girl came by to look at the crabs.
Crabby raised up his claws to protect himself
when he saw her.

But that little girl loved every living thing.
"Oh, this crab is a papershell," she said
to Capt. Mickey who was nearby.
"Please, may I let him swim free?"

"You always want to turn loose every crab,"
Capt. Mickey said. "But yes, let him go."

Quickly, Crabby swam free and
away from that

"I am going to look for Nabby," he thought.
"I know she will be at Broken Bridge Inlet
where all the 'sook' crabs go."

Crabby swam and swam until he came
to Broken Bridge Inlet beside the sea.
He found Nabby there — just as he expected.

Nabby had become a "sponge" crab and
would soon lay her eggs.
She was surprised to see Crabby!

He told her about the little girl who
was a HELPFUL HUMAN.
"You need to be more careful," Nabby said.

"Oh yes," replied Crabby.
"I'll never be a careless crab again!
I know that I've had a close call."